Two of a Kind

OKAO
PUBLISHING

Written by Kenny Onatolu   Illustrated by Steven Celiceo

Two of a Kind

Published by OKAO Publishing
Okaopublishing@gmail.com
Copyright © 2018 By Kenny Onatolu

Written by Kenny Onatolu
Illustrated by Steven Celiceo

978-0-692-98992-0

LCCN Number 2018935982

JUVENILE NONFICTION / Biography & Autobiography / Sports & Recreation
JUVENILE NONFICTION / Religious / Christian / Social Topics

OKAO
PUBLISHING
ELKHORN, NE

To my daughter, Amera, and sons, Knox and Kai.
You are all blessings from above.

I wish you the strength to face life's many challenges,
the wisdom to do what is right more often than not,
and passion in whatever you so choose.
Learn to give without reason and to care for people
without expecting anything in return.

Most importantly, love unconditionally,
because love is the strongest of all.

My name is Kenny Onatolu. I met my good friend, Dave, playing football. Now our sons are friends too. We tell them our old football stories and watch our tapes together.

We met during a Thursday night game when he was blocking me. Dave is a trickster. He knew we were neighbors and I didn't. So just as the ball was snapped, he distracted me by inviting me over to his house after the season. Instead of a holding penalty on him, it was a bad play for me.

He still teases me about how well he blocked me that night. But we both know what really happened. It's one of the many fun stories we've shared.

People are surprised that Dave grew up in a rough neighborhood and attended a high school surrounded by barbed wire fencing.

I spent my first six years living in Nigeria but moved back to the United States where I grew up in a family with everything I needed.

Dave saw our different skin colors as a sign of having different experiences and he started asking me questions. He asked me why my name is so long and if it means anything. That was a big deal to me because most people made fun of my name. Dave didn't.

My full name is Olayiwola Kehinde Adebowale Onatolu.

It means:
Olayiwola—Wealth
Kehinde— Twin
Adebowale—Crown is Home.

NIGERIA

Dave and I learned so much about each other because of how open we were to our differences. I liked that he asked me so many questions. It showed that he was interested and he cared.

Now our sons know about living in Nigeria and eating goat meat.

Even their friends think it tastes just like hamburger.

Dave still asks questions. He even gets his hair cut
at my barbershop because he likes talking sports and joking
with the guys. He's very comfortable there even though
he stands out because of his skin color.

It's funny to me to see his hair with the same razor cuts as mine. I am proud that he's my friend and of his openness to other people. It takes him all afternoon to get a haircut but he's having fun.

We talk to our boys about getting to know people before judging them.

Now our sons ask us questions.

I've learned not
to react like that.
In Sunday school
I learned to treat
everyone with love
even though it's
not always easy.

I teach my sons to respect themselves.

Never let anyone
make fun of who
you are as a person.

That means what
you look like,
how you talk,

or even what you eat.

Their friend may not
understand how hurtful
teasing can be.
It is their job
to teach them.

I tell my boys it's not easy to speak up when we should. I'm still practicing speaking up too.

A friend told me a story of his little boy looking at a poster of a famous black athlete and thinking it was me.

His son thinks every person with my skin color looks the same.

He thinks this way because he doesn't see many people with brown skin except for me.

I knew my friend thought it was cute and innocent...

But I wished I had the courage
to tell him he missed a perfect
opportunity to teach his son about
different types of people.

I've now learned to speak up even
if it makes people uncomfortable.
Speaking up is the right
thing to do.

I teach my boys to do the same.

Their friends may not understand
now, but someday they will.

I remember when my son first noticed his skin color was different than mine.

We were watching basketball on TV and he said, "Look at all the brown guys."

I said, "You're brown too."

That didn't make sense to him.

So he scratched his skin looking for the brown underneath. I thought that was funny but I knew it was an important question to him.

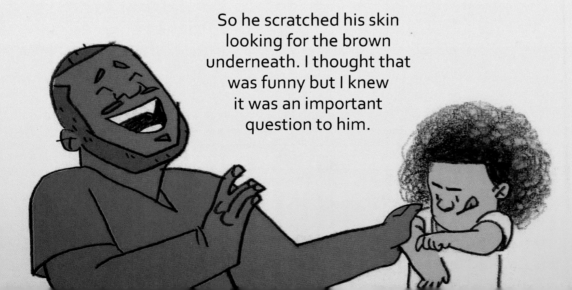

When I explained that his mother is white
and I am brown and it is like mixing
two colors of paint to make
a new color, he understood.

He says, "I'm special because
I have the best of both
worlds." I agree.

Now we hear our boys talking about being best friends and it gives us hope for the future.

Their differences don't bother them, they intrigue them.

Although we have some differences in our cultures,
we have a lot of similarities also.

That is what makes us such good friends.

You could say, we're Two of a Kind.

We get to teach each other
things we wouldn't have
known if we hadn't
become friends.

Football brought Dave and I together and that is why we love it so much. Maybe our boys will love it as much as we do someday.

Dave and I learn a lot from watching our boys play together. It reminds us that even grown ups can learn from little kids. It is important to realize that you are never too young or too old to learn or teach someone to love first. The greatest teacher was only 12 years old when He began teaching. And He changed the world.

My name is Olayiwola Kehinde Adebowale Onatolu

As an African American man raised in a community lacking diversity, I believe I have a good understanding of why we seem to be taking a step back when it comes to race relations in America. As the father of three biracial children, I have a passion for race reconciliation in the United States. It is my belief that if we can reach and teach our children while they're young, they'll be much more understanding of others when they become adults. Children are honest and ask questions that may at times make adults feel uncomfortable. Instead of answering those questions, we dismiss them. I believe answering those difficult questions about race, provides the perfect opportunity to teach lessons that will last a lifetime.

I studied communications at the University of Nebraska at Omaha where I also played football. After college I played professionally in the Canadian Football League for the Edmonton Eskimos and then in the National Football League for the Minnesota Vikings and Carolina Panthers. I love football because of the physical and mental adversity. I always enjoyed the feeling after a game when my body felt beat up. It reminded me that I had accomplished a difficult task. An injury ended my career and forced me to think about what is most important to me.

Olayiwola "Kenny" with older son Knox, son Kai, baby Amera, and wife Jessie Laree Onatolu

Faith and family are now my focus. One Sunday while teaching Sunday school, a three-year-old girl asked me why my skin was dirty and told me to stop playing in the mud. I didn't get offended or dismiss her. I took that opportunity to teach her. I simply replied, "It's just the way God made me." She smiled, said okay, and went about her day.

Acknowledgments

The completion of this book could not have been possible without the participation of a number of people. Their contributions are greatly appreciated. I would like to express my appreciation and gratitude to the following people. My wife Jessie Onatolu, my brother Taiwo Onatolu, my father Dr. Debo Onatolu, my pastor Rowlie Hutton, my friend David Tollefson, and most importantly to my father in heaven, the author of life and love.

The original "two of a kind."
Kenny Onatolu on the right with his
twin brother, Taiwo Onatolu, on the left.

The inspirations for *Two of a Kind*.
Dave Tollefson, the man of many questions, and Kenny Onatolu.

Find out more about Kenny at www.kennyonatolu.com

The next generation "two of a kind,"
Tucker Tollefson and Knox Onatolu,
who inspired Kenny to write this book.

About the Illustrator

Steven Celiceo grew up in California with a crayon in each hand. Lately he's also picked up pencils, pens, and paint and learned how to create digitally. Steven has worked in children's books, video games, and TV. He went to school at San Jose State University as well as Animation Collaborative where he trained to be a traditional artist and developed a passion for creating characters. He takes inspiration from his niece, family and friends and tries to inspire them in kind. Steven's aspiration is to be able to understand and communicate both the complexities and simplicity of human emotions. Follow him at www.celiceo.com

Made in the USA
Middletown, DE
18 June 2020